Happy birthday, Tom and Ruby,

Solve the riddles to find your presents.

"Hurray, I love riddles!" Ruby cried.

"Me too," grinned Tom.

He opened the first riddle.

"*I am full of holes but still hold water,*" he read.

"Hmm, how can something hold water if it's full of holes?" said Ruby.

Tom thought hard. "What holds water?

Cups, jugs, vases, sinks, baths ..."

"Sinks and baths have plugholes," said Ruby.

"But they're not *full* of holes," argued Tom.

"But sponges are," Ruby cried suddenly.

"And they hold water ..."

The twins raced upstairs to the bathroom.

Next to the bath sponge were two presents.

"Hurray!" Tom cried.

Chapter 2

"What a strange present," Tom said,

unwrapping a squeaky horn.

"Fun, though," Ruby grinned, squeaking hers.

"And look – another riddle.

You bought me for dinner but you never eat me,"

Ruby read, frowning.

"Why would you buy something

for dinner but not eat it?"

"Hmm," Tom said. "Maybe it's something you use

for dinner instead?"

"Like plates?" Ruby said. "Or knives and forks?"

The twins ran back downstairs and searched

the kitchen drawers and cupboards ...

13

... and found two presents in a big saucepan.

"Hurray!" Ruby cried.

The twins quickly unwrapped them.

Inside were two water bottles ...

and another riddle.

"*What goes up and down but never moves?*

Look under me," read Tom.

"If something goes up and down it has to move,

doesn't it?" said Ruby.

"Hmm, that's a tough one," said Tom, frowning.

"What goes up and down? A yo-yo? A rocket?"

"But they both move," Ruby frowned. "This one is really hard."

"I hope you two aren't going to be running up and down those stairs all day," said Dad. "Sorry, Dad," said Ruby. "Wait, that's it!"

"Stairs go up and down but never move!"

cried Ruby, running to the cupboard

under the stairs ...

Inside were two more presents.

"This is fun!" Tom laughed

as they unwrapped them.

"What great jackets," Ruby grinned,

putting hers on.

"And look, there's another riddle

in the pocket," said Tom.

20

"*I have a roof, four walls and one door*

but I am not made of bricks ..." he read.

"I know the answer!" Ruby cried.

Chapter 3

Ruby ran to her bedroom and looked

in her old doll's house.

But there were no presents inside.

"The doll's house doesn't have four walls,"

Tom said. "It only has three."

"Of course," Ruby sighed. "But then what

could be the answer?"

Suddenly, Tom's eyes lit up. "I know!"

Tom ran downstairs, then outside to the car.

"Of course!" Ruby cried. "Well done, Tom!"

The twins peered inside the car ...

but there were no presents in the car either.

"Of course, the car has four doors, not one!"

said Ruby.

"Oh, yes," Tom sighed. "But what else could have

a roof, four walls and one door but not be made

of bricks?"

Suddenly the twins looked at each other.

"I know!" they both cried.

Chapter 4

"The shed has a roof, four walls and a door,"

cried Tom, running across the garden.

"And it is not made of bricks," added Ruby.

Sure enough, there, inside the shed,

were two big presents.

"Bikes!" the twins cried.

"Of course – water bottles, squeaky horns,

waterproof jackets ..." Tom grinned.

"They all go with bikes."

"Each of the other presents was a clue

to this one!" Ruby laughed.

"Well done, Tom and Ruby," Dad said.

"Ready for a birthday bike ride?" Mum asked.

"We are now," the twins laughed.

"Thank you, Mum and Dad."

It was the best birthday ever!

Things to think about

1. Why do Tom and Ruby have to solve the riddles?
2. Did you guess where the presents might be hidden from the clues?
3. Why do you think their parents hid their presents?
4. What did you think the twins might find at the end of the story?
5. What present would you most like to receive? Why? What present would you most like to give?

Write it yourself

One of the themes of this story is celebrating a special occasion. Can you write a story with a similar theme?

Plan your story before you begin to write it.
Start off with a story map:

- a beginning to introduce the characters and where your story is set (the setting);
- a problem which the main characters will need to fix;
- an ending where the problems are resolved.

Get writing! Try to use interesting verbs, such as grinned / argued / frowned / sighed / searched / peered, to describe the action and excite your reader.

Notes for parents and carers

Independent reading
This series is designed to provide an opportunity for your child to read independently, for pleasure and enjoyment. These notes are written for you to help your child make the most of this book.

About the book
It's the twins' birthday, and their parents have left a series of riddles that they must solve to find their presents.

Before reading
Ask your child why they have selected this book. Look at the title and blurb together. What do they think it will be about? Do they think they will like it?

During reading
Encourage your child to read independently. If they get stuck on a word, remind them that they can sound it out in syllable chunks. They can also read on in the sentence and think about what would make sense.

After reading
Support comprehension and help your child think about the messages in the book that go beyond the story, using the questions on the page opposite. Give your child a chance to respond to the story, asking:

- Did you enjoy the story and why?
- Who was your favourite character?
- What was your favourite part?
- What did you expect to happen at the end?

Franklin Watts
First published in Great Britain in 2020
by The Watts Publishing Group

Series Editors: Jackie Hamley and Melanie Palmer
Series Advisors: Dr Sue Bodman and Glen Franklin
Series Designers: Cathryn Gilbert and Peter Scoulding

A CIP catalogue record for this book is
available from the British Library.

ISBN 978 1 4451 7236 1 (hbk)
ISBN 978 1 4451 7241 5 (pbk)
ISBN 978 1 4451 7247 7 (library ebook)
ISBN 978 1 4451 7904 9 (ebook)

Printed in China

Franklin Watts
An imprint of
Hachette Children's Group
Part of The Watts Publishing Group
Carmelite House
50 Victoria Embankment
London EC4Y 0DZ

An Hachette UK Company
www.hachette.co.uk

www.reading-champion.co.uk

FSC
www.fsc.org
MIX
Paper from
responsible sources
FSC® C104740